Lucy Steps Through the Wardrobe

Adapted from *The Chronicles of Narnia* by C. S. Lewis

Illustrated by Deborah Maze

HarperCollins*Publishers*

Lucy Steps Through the Wardrobe
Text adapted from *The Lion, the Witch and the Wardrobe*,
copyright © 1950 by C.S. Lewis (Pte) Limited.
Copyright renewed 1978 by C.S. Lewis (Pte) Limited.
Illustrations copyright © 1997 by HarperCollins Publishers, Inc.
Printed in the U.S.A. All rights reserved.
http://www.harperchildrens.com

Library of Congress Cataloging-in-Publication Data
Lucy steps through the wardrobe / adapted from the chronicles of
Narnia by C. S. Lewis ; illustrated by Deborah Maze.
    p.   cm.
  Summary: A girl finds her way through the back of a wardrobe
into the magic land of Narnia and meets Mr. Tumnus, a Faun, who
invites her to tea.
  ISBN 0-06-027450-6. — ISBN 0-06-027451-4 (lib. bdg.)
  [1. Fantasy.] I. Lewis, C. S. (Clive Staples), 1898–1963. Chronicles
of Narnia. II. Maze, Deborah, ill.
PZ7.L9735 1997   96-23200
[E]—dc20   CIP
                                              AC

Typography by Steve Scott
1 2 3 4 5 6 7 8 9 10
❖
First Edition

In memory of C. S. Lewis
—D. M.

Once there were four children living in London whose names were Peter, Susan, Edmund and Lucy. During the Second World War, because of the air-raids, they were sent far away into the country to stay at the house of Professor Kirke. This story is about their adventure there.

The first morning, the children decided to explore the house. It was a very large house, the kind you never seem to come to the end of, and it was full of unexpected places. One room had a suit of armor in it. Another was all in green and had a harp in the corner. And one room was entirely empty except for a big wardrobe with a looking-glass on the door.

"Nothing there!" said Peter, and they all trooped out again.

All except Lucy. She wanted to see what was inside the wardrobe, so she opened the door and stepped in. She left the door open, of course, because she knew it is very foolish to shut oneself into a wardrobe. As she pushed aside the coats, she felt something cold and crunchy under her feet, and something cold and soft on her head.

"This is very odd," she thought.

Then she felt something hard and rough against her face. "Why, it is just like branches of trees!" exclaimed Lucy.

A moment later she found that she was standing in the middle of a wood at night-time with snow under her feet and snowflakes falling through the air. Over her shoulder, Lucy could still see the open doorway of the wardrobe and a glimpse of the empty room she had come from. Ahead of her, between the dark tree-trunks, she could see a bright light shining far off in the forest.

"I can always go back if anything goes wrong," thought Lucy. She began to walk, crunch-crunch, over the snow toward the light.

When Lucy reached the light, she found it was a lamp-post. As she stood wondering what a lamp-post was doing in the middle of a wood, she heard a pitter patter of feet coming toward her. Suddenly a very strange person stepped out from among the trees. From the waist upward he was like a man. But his legs were shaped like a goat's and he had hoofs instead of feet. He was a Faun.

"Goodness gracious me!" exclaimed the Faun when he saw Lucy.

"Good evening," said Lucy.

"Good evening," said the Faun, giving her a little bow. "Excuse me—I don't mean to be rude—but are you a Daughter of Eve?"

"My name is Lucy," said Lucy, a little puzzled.

"But are you a girl?" asked the Faun. "A Human girl?"

"Of course I am," replied Lucy, thinking his questions very strange.

"I have never seen a Son of Adam or a Daughter of Eve before," said the Faun. "I am delighted to meet you! My name is Tumnus."

"I am very pleased to meet you, Mr. Tumnus," said Lucy.

"And may I ask, O Lucy Daughter of Eve," said Mr. Tumnus, "how have you come into Narnia?"

"Narnia? What is Narnia?" said Lucy.

"This is Narnia," said the Faun. "All the land between the lamp-post and the great castle of Cair Paravel. And how have you come here?"

"I got in through the wardrobe in the spare room," said Lucy.

"Ah!" said Mr. Tumnus. "If I had only worked harder at geography when I was a little Faun, I should no doubt know all about those strange countries."

"But they aren't countries at all," said Lucy, almost laughing. "It is only just back there—at least—I'm not sure. It is summer there."

"Meanwhile," said Mr. Tumnus, "it is winter in Narnia, and has been for ever so long. We shall both catch cold if we stand here talking in the snow. Lucy, Daughter of Eve, from the fair city of War Drobe, in the far land of Spare Oom, will you come and have tea with me?"

"Thank you very much," said Lucy, who was feeling a little hungry. "But I can't stay long. I should be getting back soon."

"My cave is only just around the corner," said the Faun. "And if you will take my arm, I shall be able to hold this umbrella over both of us."

And so Lucy found herself walking arm in arm with Mr. Tumnus as if they had known each other all their lives.

They had not gone far before Mr. Tumnus led Lucy into one of the nicest caves she had ever seen. There was a carpet on the dry stone floor and two little chairs. Lucy and the Faun sat in the chairs next to a cheerful fire and had a wonderful tea. There was a nice brown egg, lightly boiled, for each of them, then sardines on toast, then buttered toast, then toast and honey, and finally a sugar-topped cake.

When Lucy couldn't eat a bite more, the Faun began to tell her wonderful tales about life in the forest. He told her about the Nymphs who lived in the wells and the Dryads who lived in the trees. He told her about the milk-white stag who could give you wishes if you caught him. He told her about the treasures of the Red Dwarfs who lived in caverns far beneath the forest floor. Then he took out a little flute and began to play a tune that made Lucy want to cry and laugh and dance and go to sleep all at the same time.

Finally Lucy said, "Oh, Mr. Tumnus—I'm so sorry to stop you—but really, I must go home."

"It's no good *now*," said the Faun, shaking his head at her sadly.

Lucy noticed that the Faun's brown eyes had filled with tears. Then the tears were trickling down his cheeks, and soon they were running off the end of his nose. At last the Faun covered his face with his hands and began to sob.

"Mr. Tumnus!" said Lucy. "What is the matter? Aren't you well? Dear Mr. Tumnus, do tell me what is wrong." And she gave him her handkerchief.

The Faun just took the handkerchief and kept on using it, wringing it with both hands whenever it got too wet. Soon Lucy was standing in a damp patch.

"Mr. Tumnus," shouted Lucy in his ear. "Stop it at once! You ought to be ashamed of yourself, a great big Faun like you. What on earth are you crying about?"

"I am crying because I am such a bad Faun," said Mr. Tumnus. "I am in the pay of the White Witch."

"The White Witch? Who is she?" asked Lucy.

"Why, it is she who has got all Narnia under her thumb. It's she who makes it always winter and never Christmas. Think of that!"

"How awful!" said Lucy. "But what does she pay *you* for?"

"I am a kidnapper for her," sobbed Mr. Tumnus. "I had orders from the White Witch that if ever I saw a Son of Adam or a Daughter of Eve, I was to catch it and hand it over to her. And you are the first I ever met. And I've pretended to be your friend and asked you to tea, and all the time I've been planning to wait for you to fall asleep, so I could go tell *Her*."

"Oh, but you won't, Mr. Tumnus," said Lucy. "You won't, will you? Indeed, you really mustn't!"

"And if I don't," said Mr. Tumnus, "she is sure to find out. And she will be very angry and wave her wand and turn me into stone so that I shall be only a statue of a Faun in her horrible house!"

"I am very sorry, Mr. Tumnus," said Lucy. "But please let me go home."

"Of course I will," said the Faun. "I hadn't known what Humans were like before I met you. I can't give you up to the Witch; not now that I know you. But we must leave at once, before she finds out you have been here," he continued. "And we must go as quietly as we can. The whole wood is full of *her* spies. Even some of the trees are on her side."

So Mr. Tumnus and Lucy went out into the snow. They stole along as quickly as they could, always keeping to the darkest places. At last they reached the lamp-post.

"I can see the wardrobe door!" Lucy said, feeling relieved.

"Then go home as quickly as you can," said the Faun, "and can you ever forgive me for what I meant to do?"

"Why, of course I can," said Lucy. "And I do hope you don't get into any trouble on my account."

"Farewell, Daughter of Eve," said Mr. Tumnus. "Perhaps I may keep the handkerchief?"

"Of course! Good-bye!" called Lucy, running toward the wardrobe door.

Soon, instead of rough branches brushing against her face Lucy felt coats. Then she felt wooden boards under her feet instead of snow. All at once she found herself jumping out of the wardrobe into the same empty room where the adventure had begun.

"I'm here!" she shouted. "I'm here. I've come back, I'm all right!"

Lucy ran into the hall and found the other three children standing there.

"It's all right," she said, "I've come back!"

"What are you talking about, Lucy?" said Susan.

"Come back?" said Peter.

"Batty," said Edmund, tapping his head. "Quite batty."

So Lucy told them she had gone through the magic wardrobe into Narnia, where there was a Faun and a witch and a mysterious lamp-post. But the other three didn't believe her. And strangely, when Lucy showed the others the wardrobe, all they found, to Lucy's dismay, was a perfectly ordinary wardrobe, with a perfectly ordinary back to it. After that, there was nothing Lucy could say to convince the others that she was telling the truth.

But of course Lucy *was* telling the truth. And although the children didn't know it then, their adventures in Narnia were just beginning.